ALIEN KIDNAP

TONY BRADMAN JAKE HILL

EDGE FRANKLIN WATTS

LONDON·SYDNEY

Franklin Watts
First published in Great Britain in 2019 by The Watts Publishing Group

Series Editor: Adrian Cole
Project Editor: Katie Woolley
Designer: Cathryn Gilbert
Illustrations: Jake Hill

HB ISBN 978 1 4451 5638 5
PB ISBN 978 1 4451 5639 2
Library ebook ISBN 978 1 4451 6358 1

Printed in China

MIX
Paper from
responsible sources
FSC
www.fsc.org   FSC® C104740

Franklin Watts
An imprint of
Hachette Children's Group
Part of The Watts Publishing Group
Carmelite House
50 Victoria Embankment
London EC4Y 0DZ

An Hachette UK Company
www.hachette.co.uk

www.franklinwatts.co.uk

Layla   Jayden   Caleb

They are…

HUMMMMM!

9

"First, I will study your brains!" shouted the emperor.

"I don't like the sound of that!" said Jayden.

"I'll be back after dinner," said Emperor
of the Vordar.

"Take your time!" shouted Layla.

16

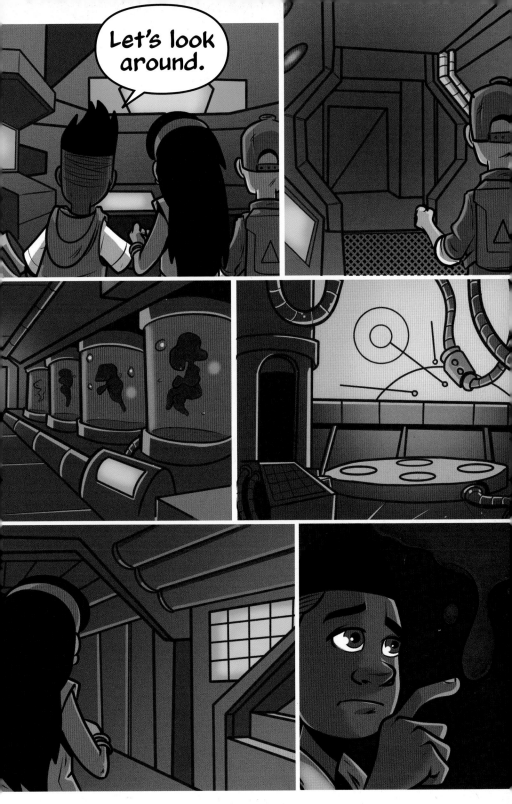

20

Kid Force 3 are surrounded by
hundreds of guards.

"We're in trouble," shouted
Jayden. "Here they come!"

ZAPPP!

WHOOOOSH!

CLANGGGG!

This way!

30